The Love Story of
Apollo and Daphne

Mythology gives you interesting explanations about life and satisfies your curiosity with stories that have been made up to explain surprising or frightening phenomena. People throughout the world have their own myths. In the imaginary world of mythology, humans can become birds or stars. The sun, wind, trees, and the rest of the natural world are full of gods who often interact with humans.

Greek and Roman mythology began more than 3,000 years ago. It consisted of stories first told by Greeks that lived on the shores of the Mediterranean Sea. In Italy the Romans would later borrow and modify many of these stories.

Most of the Greek myths were related to gods that resided upon the cloud-shrouded Mount Olympus. These clouds frequently could create a mysterious atmosphere on Mount Olympus. The ancient Greeks thought that their gods dwelt there and had human shapes, feelings, and behavior. The Greeks and the Romans built temples, offered animal sacrifices, said prayers, performed plays, and competed in sports to please their humanlike gods on Mount Olympus.

How did the world come into being in the first place?
Why is there night and day?
How did the four seasons come into existence?
Where do we go after we die?

Reading Greek and Roman mythology can help you understand ancient human ideas about our world. Since many Western ideas originated with the Greeks and Romans, you will benefit from taking a look into the mythology that helped to shape those important classical cultures. Understanding their mythology will give you an interesting view of the world you live in.

Apollo and Daphne

Apollo

He was the son of Zeus and the father of Orpheus. Apollo was the god of prophecy, medicine, archery, and music. He was also the twin brother of the goddess Artemis, the goddess of the moon and hunt. Apollo was regarded as the most gorgeous god. By the malice of Eros, he fell in love with Daphne; however, she fled away from him.

Daphne

She was a river nymph and the daughter of Peneus, the god of the river. Daphne was struck with one of Eros's arrows, which caused her to hate Apollo. She continued her flight from Apollo until she was turned into a laurel tree.

Eros

Eros, the god of love, was the son of Aphrodite, the goddess of beauty. Upset by Apollo's insulting remarks, Eros shot two different arrows at Apollo and Daphne, making Apollo suffer from the pain of a miserable love.

Peneus

He was the river god and the father of Daphne. Although Peneus wanted Daphne to marry Apollo, he accepted her plea to transform her into a tree.

Orpheus and Eurydice

Orpheus

Orpheus, the son of Apollo, was a talented musician. His lovely wife, Eurydice, died, but Orpheus eventually saved his wife by playing his lyre to charm the god of the Underworld.

Eurydice

She was the wife of Orpheus. In her hurry to escape from Aristaeus, a shepherd, Eurydice got bitten by a poisonous snake and died.

Aristaeus

Aristaeus was an ugly shepherd. His chase after Eurydice led her to tread on a snake and die.

Hades and Persephone

They were the king and queen of the Underworld. Hades, brother of Zeus, abducted Persephone, daughter of Demeter, to have her as his wife.

This book contains the love stories of Apollo and Daphne and of Orpheus and Eurydice.

Story One

After killing many evil monsters, Apollo became arrogant. He made fun of Eros and hurt his pride. In revenge, angry Eros shot two different arrows at Apollo and Daphne. As a result, Apollo fell madly in love with Daphne. However, she didn't reciprocate his love. Finally, her father changed her into a laurel tree so that she could escape from Apollo's advances.

Would it be an indescribable sadness if someone whom you loved deeply did not return your love?

Story Two

On his eleventh birthday, Orpheus was presented by his father Apollo with a lyre. He played it to such perfection that he even excelled Apollo, the god of music. Orpheus' enthusiasm for playing the lyre gave way at the moment he saw Eurydice. He fell in love with her. With the blessings bestowed by many gods, they tied the knot. However, their happiness didn't last long, because Eurydice died of a snake's bite. How could Orpheus overcome the sadness of losing Eurydice?

While the love story of Eros and Psyche is between a god and a human, the above two love stories are between gods. The love affairs of Greek gods involve as much sadness and pain as human love. However, the sufferings and travails of love also lead to beautiful endings.

Then, what happened to the love of Apollo and Daphne and of Orpheus and Eurydice? Let's find it out together.

Contents

Apollo and Daphne

A long time ago,
there lived
a great god
named Apollo.

Apollo often walked
from land to land
in search of adventure.
He was very brave and
killed many evil monsters
with his bow and arrows.
Unfortunately, he became
arrogant of his skill
with his bow.

Apollo

One day Apollo saw Eros practicing with a
bow and arrows.

 "Why do you play with such dangerous
things?" Apollo asked.
"You will only hurt yourself with them.
Go and play with your toys!"
Eros was very angry.

A few days later, Eros stood on a rock of
Mt. Parnassus.

He saw Apollo.

'You think you're so clever! I'll teach you a
lesson!' thought Eros.

Eros quickly pulled out a magical golden
arrow and shot it deep into Apollo's chest.

The magical arrow made Apollo fall in love
with the first woman he saw.
So when Apollo saw the nymph Daphne,
he fell in love with her.

Eros pulled out another magical arrow.
But this one was made of lead.
He shot it right through Daphne's heart.
This caused her to lose all interest in men
forever.

14

Apollo ran to the nearest meadow to collect flowers for Daphne.

And he also stopped by the nearest pond to check that his hair was neat.

Then, he ran to meet his love.

When he found her, he knelt down.

"My lady, I have brought you these flowers to show my love for you.

Please take them and let me be your husband," said Apollo.

Daphne dumped the flowers on Apollo's head.

Laughing loudly, she ran off into the woods. Apollo didn't know that Daphne could never love him.

Daphne was the
daughter of the
river god, Peneus.
She grew up
near many
great rivers and
mountains.
Her father taught her
how to live in the woods.
She only loved nature and didn't care about
the rest of the world.
Besides her father, Daphne had never seen
another man.

Daphne spent her
time running in
the woods and
sleeping under
the stars.

Even though
she was wild,
Apollo wanted
to marry her.
He brought her
beautiful
flowers and
delicious food
everyday.

But with a wild laugh, she stepped on
everything he brought her.
Apollo would chase her in the woods, but
she always ran faster.
He would sing songs to her, but she would

cover her ears.
He would beg her
to marry him,
but she would
kick sand in his
face.

Daphne's father saw the mighty Apollo
chasing after his daughter.
He noticed that she always rejected Apollo.
But Peneus felt that Apollo would make a
great husband for his daughter.

"Daughter," said Peneus,
one day,
"I want you to get
married.
I would like to have
a son-in-law
and grandchildren.
I think it's time
you found a
husband.
What about Apollo?
I think he would be
perfect for you."

"I'll never marry any man," replied Daphne.
"My true love is only nature and freedom."
"You are too beautiful to live alone.
Apollo will never stop chasing you,"
said Peneus.
"Then my only hope is that I can run faster
than him," she replied.
"If I can't get away from him,
please turn me into a tree
or a rock.
Then, Apollo
will forget
about me
and
I could be
alone in the
woods,
forever."

No matter how hard Apollo tried,
he could never reach Daphne.
Whenever he tried to talk to
her, she would run away.
The more she ran away,
the more he loved her.

One day as Apollo was chasing
Daphne, he shouted,
"Stop running, my love.
I am not a peasant!
I'm a god!
I have fought great battles.
And I am the greatest archer ever.
How come you don't want to marry me?
I will not stop running until I have caught
you."
"I will never let you catch me.
I love my freedom more than I could ever
love you," said Daphne.

The
chase continued
for a long time.
They ran over mountains,
through valleys, along rivers
and across great plains.
Daphne was a great runner,
but Apollo was stronger.
Little by little he got closer to her.

When Apollo was very close, Daphne began to pray.
"Dear Peneus, please help me.
Apollo will catch me soon.
Open up the ground and hide me in it.
Or change me into a tree or a rock!"

Daphne changing into a tree

As soon as she finished praying,
she suddenly stopped moving.
Daphne's arms were stiff and brown.
They looked like branches.
Her fingers were broad and green.
They looked like leaves.
Her body was thick, brown and covered
with bark.
It looked like a tree trunk.
Her feet were planted in the ground.
They looked like roots.
Daphne had become a tree!

Apollo looked at Daphne in amazement.
Apollo touched the tree bark where her
arm once was.
Daphne tried to pull her arm away,
but she couldn't.
He kissed the bark of the tree trunk.

"My love, Daphne," Apollo said, "from this moment on, I will sing to you every day and every night.

I will hang lovely bracelets on your branches and I will decorate your tree trunk.

I promise that I will love you and be with you forever."

The god Apollo then sat down beside the tree.

He took a lyre from inside his coat.

He began to play a song and sing softly to the tree.

Even today, you may hear the sound of
gentle music in some dark forest.
That is the sound of Apollo singing to his
one true love, a tree named 'Daphne'.

Orpheus and Eurydice

Orpheus was the son of Apollo.
Like Apollo, he had a great musical
talent.

One day, Apollo decided to give him a lyre.
Apollo spent weeks making this instrument.
He used the finest trees and wild horse
hairs.
He spent months decorating it and years
adjusting it.

Apollo finally finished the instrument for
Orpheus's tenth birthday.

He gave the lyre to the boy as a birthday
gift.

"Oh, thank you, father,"
said Orpheus with a big smile.

"I will treasure this lyre forever and I will
play it everyday."

Orpheus played that lyre everyday.

He became an excellent musician.

Some people said that he was even better

than his father, the god of music.

When Orpheus played,

people tapped their feet.

Birds would sing along and dogs would howl.

Even the fiercest lion would shake its head

or wave its tail with the rhythm.

30

But the music had the greatest effect on
women.
Orpheus was surrounded by them most of
the time.
They all wanted to be his girlfriend.
But he was absorbed in his music and
never paid any attention to them.

One day, Orpheus became tired of all these women.

He jumped a fence and ran into the woods to escape.

He crossed a stream and came into a wide, empty meadow.

He sat in the shade of an oak tree.

The view was so beautiful that he made a song about it.

He sang the most beautiful song in the world.

After awhile, Orpheus found that the birds were singing.

Frogs were croaking and crickets were dancing.

A young woman named Eurydice stopped
to listen.

Orpheus looked up from his lyre.

She was so beautiful that he forgot about
his music for the first time in his life.

He missed a note.

He looked at her long,

golden hair and her delicate, pale face.

He wanted to sing about her beauty.

He instantly created a new song and sang.

It was the most charming song that
Eurydice had ever heard.
It was full of emotion and tenderness.
When she heard the song,
she fell in love with the musician.
As for Orpheus, he had fallen in love the
moment that he saw Eurydice.
They were soon married.
Their wedding was in the same meadow
where they had first met.

They lit the meadow with torches.

But it was windy.

Smoke blew everywhere, even into the eyes
of the guests and the bride and groom.

Tears came from the eyes of every person
and god in the meadow.

Many people felt uncomfortable.

It was considered bad luck for people to cry
at a wedding.

A month later, Eurydice walked through
the forest one day.
Aristaeus, a shepherd,
saw the pretty young woman.
"Hello, beautiful. I suppose you've come here
to spend some time with me," said Aristaeus.
He winked at Eurydice.
This shepherd was not handsome.
He had three teeth in his mouth and two
lumps on his head.

"Come here, my beauty, and give me a kiss," he said. Aristaeus tried to put his arms around her.
Eurydice ran screaming into the woods.

"Wait, my darling. I just want a kiss," said Aristaeus.
"Aaaaaahhhhh," was her reply.

The shepherd chased her while blowing kisses. Suddenly Eurydice stepped on a snake and was bitten. In seconds, the young beauty died.

When Orpheus heard the news,
his heart was broken.
He was so sad that he couldn't speak.
He could only pick up his lyre and sing a
sad song. Then he played another sad song,
and another.
He played such sad songs that the clouds
began to weep. The mice in the fields hugged
each other for comfort. Even bears began to
beat their chest with sadness.

Then, a happy thought occurred to
Orpheus.
If he played with enough sadness,
perhaps he could bring his wife back.
Perhaps the gods in the underworld would
give her back.
Everything that lived on the earth was
affected by his music.
But no god in the sky or under the ground
could hear him.

Since Eurydice was
in the underworld,
Orpheus decided to
go there.
When Orpheus
arrived at
the river Styx,
he gently persuaded
the ferryman with a
song.

Soon he was carried across the river.

When he reached
the three-headed
dog that protects
Hades's gate,
he played a
relaxing song.
The dog fell into
a deep sleep.

Orpheus Kneeling in front of Hades and Persephone

When Orpheus stood before Hades and
Persephone, he fell to his knees.
"Welcome, Orpheus," Hades said.
"Rise and sing to us about why you have
come."

Orpheus sadly sang the following words:

"O good Hades,
We all must return to you.
When I die, I will come back
To the underworld, too.

My wife Eurydice,
Has been taken from me
By a snake's tooth.
It is as cruel as it could be.

You have taken my wife
While she is still in her prime.
This beautiful young woman
Has died before her time.

When she is old,
She will come again.
But for now, she belongs above,
In the land of men.

I cannot go on,
Separated from my wife.
A life spent alone
Is such a lonely life."

As he sang, Hades and Persephone began to shed tears. Every note was full of emotion. Every word was so honest.

The god of the underworld could not help but be moved.

Wiping the tears from his face, Hades said, "It is a pity that Eurydice died so young. I will allow you to take her into the world again."

"But there is one condition," Hades said. "You must not look at her until you've left the underworld."

Eurydice came from among the ghosts, limping with her wounded foot.

Orpheus was leading Eurydice and
Eurydice was following him.
Without looking at each other,
they walked
towards the earth.
First, they walked past the three-headed dog.
Then they crossed the river Styx.

Finally they reached
the last part of the trail.
Orpheus was not sure that she was still
following him.
But he remembered the god Hades's words.
So he couldn't look back to see his wife.

When they had nearly
reached the top,
Eurydice slipped upon
a loose rock.
She screamed with
fright.

Orpheus was so
anxious about
Eurydice.
So he turned to
look at her.
As soon as their eyes
met, Eurydice
disappeared from
Orpheus's sight.
The couple did not
even have a moment to
say goodbye.

Eurydice Disappearing From Orpheus

Orpheus immediately went back to the
underworld to follow her.

At the river Styx, the ferryman would not
listen to his pleas.

When Orpheus sang his sad songs, the
man plugged his ears with cotton.

For seven days,
Orpheus stayed on
the bank of the
river and sang
sorrowful
songs.

But the ferryman would not listen to him.
After some time,
Orpheus's songs became bitter.
Orpheus knew that no one was listening to
his songs.

When he got home, he was bitter and angry.
Orpheus no longer sang songs about the
beauty of nature or of love.
Instead,
he sang of bitter fate and unfair gods.

One day, a group of beautiful women sat
down beside the musician.

"Please, Orpheus," said one of these women.
"Play something special for us like you
used to.
It's a sad and dull life without your happy
melodies.
Why can't you just forget Eurydice for a
little while?
Are we not as beautiful and charming as
your wife?"
"WHAT?" shouted Orpheus, "as beautiful
and charming as my wife? No!"

One woman became
very angry.
She picked up a
broomstick, and hit
him over the head as
hard as she could.
Orpheus immediately
collapsed to the
ground.

15

After a few moments,
Orpheus opened his eyes.
He expected to see an angry woman
staring down at him.
Instead, he saw his wife, Eurydice.
In the underworld, the lovers were
together again.
In her arms,
Orpheus forgot about
his bitterness.

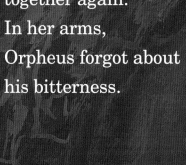

54

He forgot the angry songs he sang before.
He could only remember that he was happy.
And so, from that day,
he could only sing happy songs.

That is why the underworld is
now full of happy,
sweet melodies.

Appendixes

Reading Comprehension

Apollo and Daphne ▸▹

○ Read and answer the questions.

1. What did the magical golden arrow do to Apollo?

   (A) It made him forget about Eros.
   (B) It made him fall in love with the first
       woman that he saw.
   (C) It made him kill evil monsters.
   (D) It made him shoot straight.

2. What did the lead arrow do to Daphne?

   (A) It made her loose all interest in men,
       forever.
   (B) It made her run into the forest.
   (C) It made her beautiful.
   (D) It made her laugh loudly in the woods.

3. Why did Peneus want Daphne not to run away from Apollo?

(A) Because Peneus wanted to marry someone suitable.
(B) Because Peneus felt rejected.
(C) Because Peneus was worried about his grandchildren.
(D) Because Peneus felt that Apollo was a good match for Daphne.

4. At the end of the story, what happened to Daphne?

_____

_____

Part 2 Orpheus and Eurydice ▶▶

○ Read and answer the questions.

1. What gift did Orpheus get on his tenth birthday?

    (A) A fine tree.

    (B) A set of golf clubs.

    (C) A lyre.

    (D) Wild horse hairs.

2. How did Eurydice die?

    (A) She fell off a cliff.

    (B) She starved to death.

    (C) She died from a disease.

    (D) She died from a snakebite.

3. Why did Orpheus think that he had to go to the underworld?

    (A) Because Eurydice was lonely.

    (B) Because he wanted to make dead people cry.

(C) Because he wanted to persuade Hades to give him his wife back.

(D) Because the gods of the underworld like music.

4. What was the one condition for allowing Orpheus to take Eurydice back?

(A) Orpheus could not look at Eurydice until they had left the underworld.

(B) They could not walk past the three-headed dog.

(C) They could not hold hands.

(D) Orpheus could never again play music.

5. What happened after Orpheus was hit over the head with a broomstick?

○ Read and talk about it.

. . . When Apollo was very close, Daphne began
to pray.
"Dear Peneus, please help me. Apollo will catch
me soon.
Open up the ground and hide me in it. Or change
me into a tree or a rock!"
As soon as she finished praying, she suddenly
stopped moving.
. . . Daphne had become a tree!. . .

1. Because of Daphne's praying, Peneus made
   his daughter change into a tree.
   What would you have done if you were
   Peneus?

. . . She screamed with fright.
Orpheus was so anxious about Eurydice. So he
turned to look at her. As soon as their eyes met,
Eurydice disappeared from Orpheus's sight. The
couple did not even have a moment to say
goodbye.. . .

2. Eurydice disappeared because Orpheus
   turned to look at her.
   What would you have done if you were
   Orpheus?

_____

_____

_____

_____

The Signs of the Zodiac

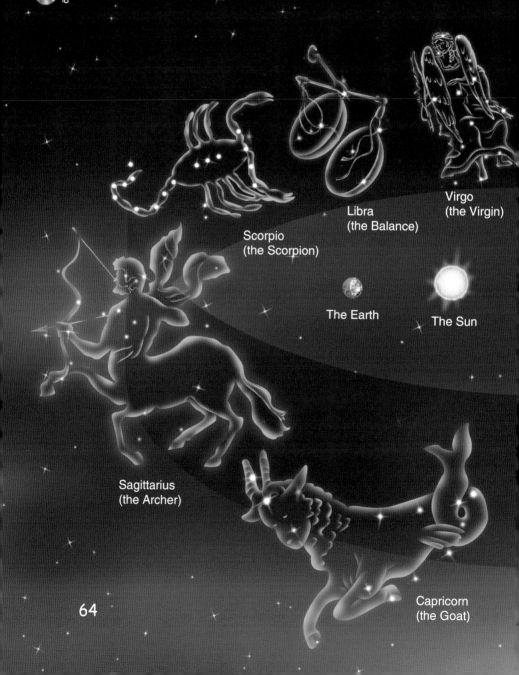

16

Scorpio
(the Scorpion)

Libra
(the Balance)

Virgo
(the Virgin)

The Earth

The Sun

Sagittarius
(the Archer)

Capricorn
(the Goat)

The word 'zodiac' comes from a Greek word meaning,
"the circle of animals".
Where did the zodiac come from?
In this section, you can find the Greek Myths
that explain the origins of these signs.

Leo
(the Lion)

Cancer
(the Crab)

Gemini
(the Twins)

Taurus
(the Bull)

Aries
(the Ram)

Pisces
(the Fishes)

Aquarius
(the Water Bearer)

65

Aries (the Ram)

March 21st ~ April 20th

The origin of Aries stems from the Tale of the Golden Ram. The ram safely carried off Phrixus.

Phrixus sacrificed the Golden Ram to Zeus and in turn, Zeus placed the ram in the heavens.

Taurus (the Bull)

April 21st ~ May 20th

The origin of Taurus stems from the Tale of Europa and the Bull. Zeus turned himself into a bull in order to attract Europa to him.

The bull carried Europa across the sea to Crete.

In remembrance, Zeus placed the image of the bull in the stars.

Gemini (the Twins)

May 21st ~ June 21st

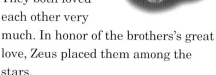

This sign stems from the Tale of Castor and Pollux. Castor and Pollux were twins. They both loved each other very much. In honor of the brothers's great love, Zeus placed them among the stars.

Cancer (the Crab)

June 22nd ~ July 22nd

The sign of Cancer stems from one of the 12 Labors of Hercules.

Hera sent the crab to kill Hercules. But Hercules crushed the crab under his foot just before he defeated the Hydra. To honor the crab, Hera placed it among the stars.

Leo (the Lion)

July 23rd ~ August 22nd

The sign of Leo stems from another of Hercules 12 Labors. Hercules°Øs the first labor was to kill a lion that lived in Nemea valley. He killed the Nemea lion with his hands. In remembrance of the grand battle, Zeus placed the Lion of Nemea among the stars.

Libra (the Balance)

September 23rd ~ October 21st

The Libra are the scales that balance justice. They are held by the goddess of divine justice, Themis. Libra shines right beside Virgo which represents Astraea, daughter of Themis.

Virgo (the Virgin)

August 23rd ~ September 22nd

Virgo°Øs origin stems from the Tale of Pandora. Virgo represents the goddess of purity and innocence, Astraea. After Pandora opened the

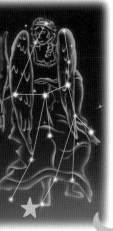

forbidden box and let loose all the evils into the world, every god went back to heaven. As a remembrance of innocence lost, Astraea was placed amongst the stars in the form of Virgo.

Scorpio (the Scorpion)

October 22nd ~ November 21st

The sign of Scorpio stems from the Tale of Orion. Orion and Artemis were great hunting partners, which made Artemis's brother Apollo very jealous. Apollo pleaded with Gaea to kill Orion. So Gaea created the scorpion and killed great Orion. In remembrance of this act, Zeus placed Orion and the scorpion amongst the stars. But they never appear at the same time.

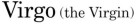

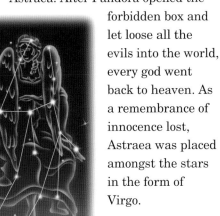

67

Sagittarius(the Archer)

November 23rd ~ December 21st

This sign is representative of

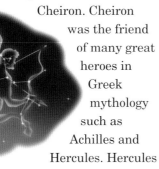

Cheiron. Cheiron was the friend of many great heroes in Greek mythology such as Achilles and Hercules. Hercules accidentally shot Cheiron in the leg with a poison arrow. Cheiron was immortal so he couldn't die. Instead, he had to endure the unending pain. Cheiron begged Zeus to kill him. To honor Cheiron, Zeus placed him among the stars.

 20

Capricorn(the Goat)

December 22nd ~ January 19th

The sign of Capricorn represents the goat Amalthea who fed the infant Zeus. It's said that Zeus placed her among the stars in gratitude.

Aquarius
(the Water Bearer)

January 20th ~ February 18th

The sign of Aquarius stems from the Tale of the Deucalion's Flood. In this tale, Zeus pours all the waters of the heavens onto earth to wash away all the evil creatures. Deucalion and his wife Pyrrha were the only survivors of the great flood.

Pisces(the Fishes)

February 19th ~ March 20th

The Pisces represents the goddess of love & beauty, Aphrodite and her son the god of love, Eros. They were taking a stroll down the Euphrates River when there was a Typhon. They pleaded for Zeus to help them escape, so Zeus changed them into fish and they swam away safely. In remembrance of this, Aphrodite is the big fish constellation and Eros is the small fish constellation.

希臘羅馬神話故事 ❽

阿波羅和達芙妮 Apollo and Daphne

First Published April, 2011
First Printing April, 2011

Original Story by Thomas Bulfinch
Rewritten by David O'Flaherty
Illustrated by Vova Gruzdov
Designer by Hyeonyoung Kim, Eonju No
Translated by Jia-chen Chuo

Printed and distributed by Cosmos Culture Ltd.
Tel: 02-2365-9739
Fax: 02-2365-9835
http://www.icosmos.com.tw
Publisher: Value-Deliver Culture Ltd.

The Love Story of
Apollo and Daphne

中譯解答本

卓加真　譯

神話以趣味的方式，為我們生活中的煩惱提出解釋，並滿足我們的好奇心。許多故事的編寫，都是為了解釋一些令人驚奇或恐懼的現象，因此，世界各地不同的國家、民族，都有屬於自己的神話。

希臘與羅馬神話充滿想像力，並結合了諸神與英雄們激盪人心的傳奇故事，因此特別為人所津津樂道。希臘與羅馬神話反應了真實的人類世界，因此，閱讀神話對於瞭解西方文化與思維，有極大的幫助。

這些經典故事的背景，可追溯至史前時代，但對於當代的讀者而言，它們深具魅力的法寶何在？其秘密就在於，神話能超越時空，完整地呈現人類心中的慾望。這些激盪人心的冒險故事，將帶您經歷生命中的各種重要事件：戰爭與和平、生命與死亡、善與惡，以及各種愛恨情仇。

希臘與羅馬神話裡所描繪的諸神，並不全是完美、萬能的天神，他們和人類一樣，會因憤怒而打鬥，會耍詭計戲弄其他天神，會因愛與嫉妒而感到痛苦。在 Let's Enjoy Mythology 系列的第二部 Reading Greek and Roman Mythology in English 中，你將會讀到許多具有人類特質的英雄、女英雄、眾神和女神的故事。

Reading Greek and Roman Mythology in English 將引領你穿越時空，一探想像中的古希臘世界。

前言

　　本書內容包含了「阿波羅與達芙妮的愛情故事」，以及「奧菲斯與尤麗黛的愛情故事」。

〔故事一：阿波羅與達芙妮的愛情故事〕

　　阿波羅殺死許多怪物之後，就變得驕傲自負。他嘲笑愛羅斯，並傷他的自尊心。憤怒的愛羅斯為了報復，分別對阿波羅與達芙妮射了一箭。結果，阿波羅便瘋狂地愛上了達芙妮，然而達芙妮對此卻無動於衷。後來，達芙妮的父親將她變成一株月桂樹，讓她徹底拒絕阿波羅的殷勤。假如你所深愛之人對你無動於衷，不正是一種無以名之的痛苦嗎？

〔故事二：奧菲斯與尤麗黛的愛情故事〕

　　奧菲斯十一歲生日的時候，父親阿波羅送給他一把七絃琴。奧菲斯彈奏得完美無瑕，琴藝更勝音樂之神阿波羅。但當他一見尤麗黛便為之傾心，把練琴之事全拋在腦後。於是在眾神的祝福之下，兩人結為連理。然而，幸福的日子沒過多久，尤麗黛便被毒蛇咬中而死。奧菲斯該如何平復失去尤麗黛之痛呢？

　　愛羅斯與賽姬之愛情故事是人神之戀，而這兩則愛情故事則是神與神之間的愛戀。希臘諸神之間的愛情，和人類一樣，交織著悲傷與痛苦，但是在種種的磨難與苦痛之下，依然有著美好的結局。

　　那麼「阿波羅與達芙妮」、「奧菲斯與尤麗黛」的愛情故事，又會發展出怎樣的情節呢？讓我們一同探個究竟。

目錄

阿波羅與達芙妮

p. 10

從前，有位偉大的神祇，
名為阿波羅。
阿波羅的足跡遍行各地，喜好冒險。
他非常地英勇，
有許多邪惡怪物命喪在
他的弓箭之下。
但不幸的是，
他為自己的射箭技術自滿了起來。
〔圖〕阿波羅

- **a long time ago**
  [ə lɑ:ŋ taɪm ə`goʊ]
  很久以前
- **named** [neɪm] 名為……
- **in search of** [ɪn sɜ:th əv]
  尋求……；尋找……
- **brave** [breɪv] 勇敢的
- **evil** [i:vəl] 邪惡的
- **monster** [`mɑ:nstər]
  怪物；怪獸
- **bow** [baʊ] 弓
- **arrow** [`ærəʊ] 箭
- **unfortunately**
  [ʌn`fɔ:rtʃənətli]
  可嘆的；令人遺憾的
- **arrogant** [`ærəgənt]
  妄自尊大的；傲慢的
- **skill** [skɪl] 技巧；技藝

---

p. 12

有一天，
阿波羅看到愛羅斯正在練習射箭。
「你為什麼要玩這麼危險的東西呢？」
阿波羅問。
「它們只會讓你受傷的，
去玩你的玩具吧！」
愛羅斯聽了很生氣。

- **practice with** [`præktɪs
  wɪð] 練習
- **dangerous**
  [`deɪndʒərəs] 危險的
- **hurt** [hɜ:rt] 使受傷
- **yourself** [jɔ:r`self]
  你自己
- **angry** [`æŋgri]
  發怒的；憤怒的

6

p. 13

幾天之後，
愛羅斯站在巴拿撒斯山的岩石上時，
他看見了阿波羅。
「還自以為聰明呢！
讓我來教訓你！」愛羅斯心想。
他迅速地抽出一支具有魔法的金箭，
一箭深中阿波羅的胸膛。

- **stood on** [stud ɑ:n]
  站在……之上
  (stand on的過去式)
- **mountain** [ˋmauntən] 山
- **Mt. Parnassus**
  巴拿撒斯山
- **clever** [ˋklevər] 聰明的
- **lesson** [ˋlesən] 教訓
- **quickly** [ˋkwɪkli] 迅速地
- **pulled out** [puld aut]
  抽出；拉出
- **magical** [ˋmædʒɪkəl]
  有法力的；有魔力的
- **shot** [ʃɑ:t] 射出
  (shoot的過去式)
- **chest** [tʃest] 胸膛

p. 14

神奇金箭，
會讓阿波羅愛上他所見到的第一位女
子。
因此，
當阿波羅一見到水澤女神達芬妮時，
便愛上她了。
接著愛羅斯抽出另一支箭，
這支箭是由鉛所製。
他將箭射向達芬妮的心。
這支箭會讓她對男人永遠失去興趣。

- **golden** [ˋgouldən] 黃金的
- **fall in love with**
  [fɔ:l ɪn lʌv wɪð] 愛上……
- **nymph** [nɪmf] 寧芙（山
  林水澤的仙女）（希神）
- **was made of**
  [wəz meɪd əv]
  由……製成
  (made是make的過去式)
- **lead** [led] 鉛
- **through** [θru:] 通過；穿過
- **cause** [kɔ:z]
  成為……的原因
- **lose** [lu:z] 失去
- **interest in** [ˋɪntrɪst in]
  對……有興趣
- **forever** [fərˋevə]
  永遠地；永久地

p. 15

阿波羅來到附近的草地上，
要摘花束送給達芬妮。
他還跑去附近的池塘，
去梳理自己的儀容，
然後才敢去見心愛的人。
當他找到了達芬妮，
他跪在她的跟前跟她說：
「可愛的小姐，我帶來花束，
以代表對妳的仰慕。
請收下吧，
讓我成為妳的丈夫。」阿波羅說。
達芬妮卻將花束丟在阿波羅頭上，
然後大聲笑著就跑進森林裡去了。
阿波羅不知道
達芬妮是不可能愛他的。

- **nearest** [nɪrɪst] 最近的
  （near近的；nearer較近的）
- **meadow** [`medoʊ]
  草地；牧場
- **collect** [kə`lɛkt] 收集
- **stop by** [stɑ:p baɪ]
  停留；逗留
- **pond** [pɑ:nd] 池塘
- **check** [tʃɛk] 檢查；注意
- **neat** [ni:t]
  乾淨的；整潔的
- **found** [faʊnd]
  偶然遇見；找到
  （find的過去式）
- **knelt down** [nɛlt daʊn]
  跪下
  （knelt是kneel的過去式）
- **brought** [brɔ:t]
  帶來；取來
  （bring的過去式）
- **show** [ʃoʊ] 表示
- **let** [lɛt] 允許；讓
- **husband** [`hʌzbənd] 丈夫
- **dump** [dʌmp] 倒；丟棄
- **loudly** [laʊdlə]
  高聲地；大聲地
- **ran off** [ræn ɑ:f]
  跑開；逃走
  （ran是run的過去式）

p. 16

達芬妮是河神潘紐士之女。
她在大河與山巒間長大，
父親教過她如何在森林裡生活。
她只愛大自然，
不在乎世上的其他東西。
除了父親，
達芬妮從未見過其他男人。
達芬妮喜歡在樹林間奔跑，
與星辰共眠。

- **Peneus** [puˈnèus] 潘紐士
- **grew up** [gru: ʌp]
  成熟；成長
  （grew是grow的過去式）
- **taught** [tɑ:t]
  教導；使明白
  （teach的過去式）
- **how to** [hau tə]
  如何去……
- **care about** [ker əˈbaut]
  介意……；掛心……
- **the rest of** [ðə rest əv]
  其他一切……
- **another** [əˈnʌðər]
  另一……；再一……
- **spent** [spent] 花（時間）
  渡過（spend的過去式）

----

p. 17

達芬妮雖然比較野，
但阿波羅仍舊想娶她為妻。
阿波羅每天都會為她
帶來美麗的花束和美味的食物，
但達芬妮都只會對他狂笑一聲，
然後把他送來的任何東西
都丟在地上踐踏。
阿波羅會追著她跑進森林，
卻怎麼也追趕不上。
他也會為她高唱情歌，
但她會用手搗住耳朵。
他向她求婚，
她就會把地上的沙子往他臉上踢去。

- **even though** [ˈi:vən ðou]
  即使……也……；
  雖然……還是……
- **wild** [waɪld]
  任性的；野蠻的
- **delicious** [dɪˈlɪʃəs]
  美味的
- **stepped on** [stepd ɑ:n]
  踩；踏上；粗暴對待
  （stepped是step的過去
  式）
- **chase** [tʃeɪs] 追；追趕
- **faster** [fæstər] 更快的
  （fast快速的；fastest最
  快的）
- **beg** [beg] 懇求；請求
- **kick** [kɪk] 踢

p. 18

達芬妮的父親看著偉大的阿波羅
追著女兒不放，
也注意到女兒總是拒絕阿波羅。
但父親潘紐士認為，
阿波羅會是個好丈夫。

有一天，父親說：
「女兒啊，我希望妳能結婚，
我想要女婿和孫子，
我想妳也該找個丈夫了。
妳覺得阿波羅如何呢？
我想你們會是一對佳偶。」

- **mighty** [ˈmaɪti]
  了不起的
- **notice** [ˈnoʊtɪs]
  注意到；覺察到
- **always** [ˈɔːlweɪz] 總是
- **reject** [rɪˈdʒekt] 拒絕
- **would like to**
  [wʊd laɪk tə] 想；要
  （表示喜歡、願意）
- **son-in-law** [sʌn ɪn lɔː]
  女婿
- **grandchildren**
  [ˈɡræntʃɪldrən] 孫子
- **perfect** [ˈpɜːfɪkt]
  理想的；完善的

p. 19

達芬妮回答：「我決不結婚。
我只愛大自然與自由。」
潘紐士說：
「妳這麼漂亮，不應該單身的，
況且阿波羅不會放棄追求妳的。」
達芬妮回答：「既然如此，
我唯一的希望，就是要跑得比他快。
如果我會被他逮住，
那就請你把我變成一棵樹，
或是變成一顆石頭吧。

- **too ... to** [tuː...tə]
  太……以致於……
- **freedom** [ˈfriːdəm] 自由
- **faster** [ˈfæstər] 更快速的
- **get away** [ɡet əˈweɪ]
  跑掉；逃脫
- **turn into** [ˈtɜːrn ˈɪntə]
  使變成……
- **forget about** [fərˈæɡet]
  忘掉；不再把……放在
  心上

這樣阿波羅就會忘了我，
我也能夠永遠獨自生活在森林裡了。」

🔵 p. 20

不論阿波羅怎麼跑，
他就是追趕不上達芬妮。
只要阿波羅想跟她說話，她就跑開。
但她越是如此，阿波羅便愛得越深。

一日，阿波羅追著達芬妮大喊道：
「我心愛的人啊，妳別再跑了，
我不是凡人，我是神啊！
我打過很多偉大的戰役，
是最偉大的射箭手啊。
妳為什麼不想嫁給我呢？
沒有追到妳，我是不會放棄的。」
達芬妮回答：「我永遠不會讓你追上我
的，我愛自由，更甚於愛你，」。

- **no matter how**
  [nou `mætər hau] 不論如何
- **reach** [ri:tʃ] 伸手觸及
- **whenever** [wen`evər]
  無論何時
- **the more . . . the more**
  [ðə mɔ:r...ðə mɔ:r]
  越……越……
- **peasant** [`pezənt]
  粗野的人；農民
- **fought** [fɔ:t] 打鬥
  （fight的過去式）
- **battle** [`bætl] 戰爭
- **greatest** [greɪtɪst] 最偉大的
  （great偉大的；greater較偉
  大的）
- **archer** [`ɑ:rtʃər] 弓箭手
- **ever** [`evər]
  曾經；任何時候
- **caught** [kɔ:t] 抓住；抱住
  （catch的過去式）

🔵 p. 21

他們就這樣追跑了好一陣子。
他們跑過群山，穿過河谷，
又沿著河岸，跑過草原。
達芬妮跑得很快，
但阿波羅追的更緊，

- **continue** [kən`tɪnju:] 繼續
- **valley** [`væli] 峽谷；溪谷
- **plain** [pleɪn] 平原；曠野
- **stronger** [strɑ:ŋgər]
  更強壯的（strong強壯；
  strongest最強壯的）

逐漸地，阿波羅已經越來越近她了。

眼看阿波羅越來越逼近，
達芬妮開始祈禱。
「親愛的父親，請幫助我。
阿波羅就要追上我了。
請你打開大地，將我藏匿其中，
或是將我變成樹、變成石頭吧！」
〔圖〕達芬妮變成一棵樹

----

p. 23

達芬妮一祈禱完畢，
人突然停止下來。
她的手臂變得僵硬，變成了棕色的，
看起來就像樹枝一樣。
她的手指變得寬大，
而且成了綠色的，
看起來就像樹葉一樣。
她的身體變得很粗，
覆蓋著棕色的樹皮，
看起來就像樹幹一樣。
她的雙腳伸入了地下，
看起來就像樹根一樣。
達芬妮變成了一棵樹！

- **little by little** [ˈlɪtl baɪ ˈlɪtl] 一點一點地
- **closer** [ˈkloʊzər] 更靠近的（close靠近的；closest最靠近的）
- **pray** [preɪ] 禱告；祈禱
- **hide** [haɪd] 躲藏；躲避

- **as soon as** [əz suːn əz] 一……就……
- **finish** [ˈfɪnɪʃ] 結束；終了
- **suddenly** [ˈsʌdnli] 突然地
- **stiff** [stɪf] 僵硬的；不靈活的
- **branch** [bræntʃ] 樹枝
- **broad** [brɔːd] 寬的；寬闊的
- **was covered with** [wəz ˈkʌvəd wɪð] 覆蓋住……
- **bark** [bɑːrk] 樹皮
- **trunk** [trʌŋk] 樹幹
- **plant** [plɑːnt] 栽種
- **root** [ruːt] 根
- **in amazement** [ɪn əˈmeɪzmənt] 驚訝
- **touch** [tʌtʃ] 輕觸；觸碰

阿波羅吃驚地看著達芬妮。
他摸著樹皮，
那裡曾經是她長著雙手的地方。
達芬妮想把手甩開，卻無法如願。
阿波羅親吻了樹幹上的樹皮。

- **once** [wʌns]
  曾經的；從前的
- **pull away** [pʊl əweɪ]
  拉開

p. 24

阿波羅說：「達芬妮，吾愛，
從此刻起，我要日日夜夜為妳歌唱，
我要在妳樹枝掛上美麗的花環，
裝飾妳的樹幹。
我發誓，我會永遠愛著妳、
永遠守候著妳。」
接著，阿波羅在樹旁坐了下來，
他從長袍中拿出七弦琴，
對著樹，輕柔地彈唱著歌曲。

- **from this moment on**
  [frəm ðɪs ˋməʊmənt ɑːn]
  從此刻起
- **hang** [hæŋ] 懸掛
- **lovely** [ˋlʌvli]
  討人喜愛的；漂亮的
- **bracelet** [ˋbreslɪt] 手鐲
- **decorate** [ˋdekəreɪt]
  給……加以裝飾
- **promise** [ˋprɑːmɪs]
  向……保證
- **beside** [bɪˋsaɪd]
  在……旁邊
- **lyre** [laɪə] 里拉
  （古希臘的一種豎琴）
- **took...from** [tʊk frəm]
  從……取出
  （took是take的過去式）
- **inside** [ɪnˋsaɪd]
  內部的；裡面的
- **softly** [sɑːftlɪ]
  溫柔地；溫和地
- **gentle** [ˋdʒentl] 輕柔的
- **forest** [ˋfɔːrɪst] 森林

p. 25

時至今日，有時，
你會聽到幽暗森林中傳來輕柔的音樂，
那就是阿波羅正在對著摯愛唱歌，
他的摯愛
就是一棵名為「達芬妮」的樹。

13

一　奧菲斯與尤麗黛

p. 28

奧菲斯是阿波羅之子。
他和阿波羅一樣，擁有音樂天賦。
一日，阿波羅決定送給他一把七弦琴，
阿波羅花了數週的時間來製作這把七弦琴，
他用最上等的樹材和野馬的鬃毛，
並花了數個月的時間來裝飾樂器，
還花了數年的時間，為其調音。

* **musical** [ˋmjuːzɪkəl] 音樂的；
* **talent** [ˋtælənt] 天資；天賦
* **decide to** [dɪˋsaɪd tə] 決定去……
* **instrument** [ˋɪnstrəmənt] 樂器
* **finest** [faɪnɪst] 極好的；絕佳的（fine美好的；finer較好的）
* **horse hair** [hɔːs heə] 馬鬃
* **decorate** [ˋdekəret] 裝飾；修飾
* **adjust** [əˋdʒʌst] 調整

p. 29

最後，在奧菲斯十歲時，
阿波羅終於完成了七弦琴。
他將七弦琴送給奧菲斯，
作為生日禮物。
「感謝你，父親。」奧菲斯開心的說。
「我會永遠珍愛這把琴，
天天彈奏它。」

* **finally** [ˋfaɪnəli] 最後；終於
* **tenth** [tenθ] 第十的
* **birthday** [ˋbɜːθdeɪ] 生日
* **treasure** [ˋtreʒər] 珍視

p.30

奧菲斯每天練習，
成爲了一位偉大的音樂家。
有人說，
他甚至比身爲音樂之神的父親，
更青出於藍。
聽到奧菲斯的演奏，
人們會用腳打著拍子應和，
鳥兒會跟著唱和，狗會跟著汪汪叫，
就連最兇猛的獅子，
也會跟著節奏搖頭擺尾。

- **excellent** [ˋɛksələnt]
  卓越的；一流的
- **musician** [mjuˋzɪʃən]
  音樂家
- **even** [ˋiːvən] 即使
- **even better** [ˋiːvən ˋbɛtər]
  更勝於……
- **tap** [tæp] 輕拍
- **sing along** [sɪŋ əˋlɑːŋ]
  一起唱
- **howl** [haʊl] 對……吼叫
- **fiercest** [fɪəsɪst]
  最兇猛的（fierce 可怕
  的；fiercer 更可怕的）
- **shake** [ʃeɪk] 搖擺
- **with the rhythm** [wɪə ðə
  ˋrɪðəm] 跟著節奏

----

p. 31

他的音樂對女人來說，最是好聽。
他總是被女人所包圍，
女人們都想當他的紅粉知己，
但是他卻只沉浸在自己的音樂中，
從沒對她們多加留意。

- **effect on** [ɪˋfɛkt ɑːn]
  對……引起變化
- **was surrounded by**
  [wəz səˋraʊndɪd baɪ]
  被……包圍
- **most of the time**
  [məʊst əv ðə taɪm]
  大部分的時間
- **girlfriend** [ˋgɜːlfrɛd]
  女朋友
- **was absorbed in**
  [wəz əbˋsɔːbd ɪn]
  全神貫注在……

15

- **paid attention to**
  [peɪd əˋtenʃən tu]
  專心於
  （paid是pay的過去式）

p. 32

一日，奧菲斯覺得這些女人很煩人，
便跳過籬笆，逃進森林裡。
他涉過小溪，來到一片空曠的草原，
坐在橡樹樹蔭下。

眼前的景致如此迷人，
他為此作了一首曲子。
他唱出人間最美的旋律，
沒多久，他發現鳥兒跟著唱了起來，
蛙群嘓嘓叫，蟋蟀都跳起舞來了。

- **became tired of**
  [bɪˋkeɪm taɪəd əv]
  對……感到厭倦的
  （became是become的過
  去式）
- **fence** [fens] 柵欄；籬笆
- **escape** [ɪˋskeɪp] 逃開
- **cross** [krɑ:s] 跨過；越過
- **stream** [sti:m]
  流河；小河；小溪
- **came into** [keɪm ˋɪntə]
  進入……
- **wide** [waɪd] 寬闊的
- **empty** [ˋempti] 空曠的
- **in the shade** [ɪn ðə ʃeɪd]
  在樹蔭下；在陰涼處
- **oak** [əʊk] 櫟木；橡木
- **view** [vju:] 風景
- **awhile** [əˋwaɪl]
- **croak** [krəʊk] 片刻
- **cricket** [ˋkrɪkɪt] 蟋蟀

16

p. 33

一位名叫尤麗黛的年輕女子，
她停下腳步聆聽。
奧菲斯將目光從琴弦上抬起，
他看到眼前的女子如此美麗，
竟讓他生平以來
第一次忘了自己正在彈奏音樂，
他漏彈了一個音符。
他望著她那頭金色的長髮，
望著她那張細緻的白皙臉龐。
他想作首歌來歌頌她的美貌，
當下，他便譜出新曲，唱了出來。

- **listen** [ˈlɪsən] 傾聽
- **forgot** [fəˈgɑːt] 忘卻；忘記（forget的過去式）
- **for the first time** [fə ðə fɜːst teɪm] 第一次
- **miss** [mɪs] 漏掉
- **note** [nəʊt] 音符
- **delicate** [ˈdelɪkɪt] 細緻的；優美的
- **pale** [peɪl] 白皙的；蒼白的
- **instantly** [ˈɪnstəntli] 立即；馬上
- **create** [kriˈeɪt] 創造；創作

---

p. 34

這是尤麗黛聽過的最動人樂音了，
歌曲充滿了情感，非常的柔情。
她一聽到這歌聲，
便愛上了這位音樂家。
而奧菲斯對她也是一見傾心。
沒多久，他們就結為連理，
而婚禮舉行的地點，
就選在他們初次邂逅的草原上。

- **charming** [ˈtʃɑːmɪŋ] 迷人的；動人的
- **had ever heard** [hæd ˈevər hɜːd] 過去曾經聽過的（heard是hear的過去式）
- **be full of** [bi fʊl əv] 充滿……的
- **fell in love with** [fel ɪn lʌv wɪθ] 愛上……
- **emotion** [ɪˈməʊʃən] 感情；情緒
- **tenderness** [ˈtendənəs] 深情
- **wedding** [ˈwedɪŋ] 婚禮

p. 35

他們用火炬點亮草原，
但那天吹著風，吹得火焰的煙迷漫，
甚至薰到了賓客和新人的眼睛。
草原上，
所有凡人和神祇的眼中都泛著淚光。
很多人感到不適，
因爲人們認爲，
在婚禮上流下眼淚，
是個不祥的預兆。

- **lit** [lɪt] 點燃
  （light的過去式）
- **torch** [tɔ:rtʃ] 火炬；火把
- **blew** [blu:] 被吹向……
  （blow的過去式）
- **even into** [ˋi:vən ˋɪntə]
  甚至進到……之中
- **guest** [gest] 賓客
- **bride** [braɪd] 新娘
- **groom** [gru:m] 新郎
- **felt** [felt] 可以感覺到
  （feel的過去式）
- **uncomfortable**
  [ʌnˋkʌmftəbəl] 不舒服
- **consider** [kənˋsɪdə]
  認爲；看作
- **bad luck** [bæd]
  惡運；倒霉

p. 36

一個月後的某一天，
尤麗黛徒步走過森林。
牧羊人亞里斯陶斯看到這位美麗的年輕
婦人，
便搭訕道：「妳好啊，美人兒，
我想妳是要來陪我的吧。」
他對尤麗黛拋了拋媚眼。
這個牧羊人其貌不揚，
他嘴裡只剩三顆牙舊，
頭上還長了兩個膿包。

- **walk** [wɔ:k] 步行；散步
- **forest** [ˋfɑ:rɪst] 森林
- **shepherd** [ˋʃepəd]
  牧羊人
- **suppose** [səˋpəuz]
  假定；推測
- **wink at** [wɪŋk æt]
  眨眼示意
- **handsome** [ˋhænsəm]
  英俊；風度翩翩的
- **lump** [lʌmp] 膿包

p. 37

「來吧，美人兒，來親親我。」他說。
亞里斯陶斯想抱住尤麗黛，
尤麗黛尖聲跑進森林。
「等等，親愛的，讓我親一下嘛。」
亞里斯陶斯說。
「啊！」尤麗黛叫了一下。
牧羊人邊追，邊送著飛吻。
突然間，尤麗黛踩到一條蛇，
被蛇給咬到，
沒幾秒鐘，
這位美麗的女子便撒手人寰了。

- **scream** [skri:m] 尖叫
- **darling** [`dɑ:lɪŋ] 親愛的
- **reply** [rɪ`plaɪ]
  回應；答覆
- **blow** [bləʊ] 吹送
- **suddenly** [`sʌdnli]
  突然地
- **step on** [step ɑ:n]
  踏上；踩到
- **was bitten** [wəz `bɪtn]
  被咬
- **in seconds** [ɪn `sekəndz]
  在幾秒之間

---

p. 38

聽到愛妻的噩耗，奧菲斯柔腸寸斷。
他悲傷得無法言語，
只能拾起七弦琴，
唱著一首又一首的悲歌。
他唱的歌如此悲傷，
連白雲也開始啜泣了起來，
田野上的老鼠們互相擁抱，
以求撫慰，
就連熊隻也搥胸頓足，哀傷無比。

- **news** [nju:z] 新聞
- **was broken** [wəz
  `brəʊkən] 破裂了的
  （broken是break的過去式）
- **weep** [wi:p] 哭泣
- **mice** [maɪs] 老鼠
  （mouse的複數）
- **field** [fi:ld] 田野；野外
- **hugged** [hʌgd] 擁抱
- **comfort** [`kʌmfət] 舒適的
- **chest** [tʃest] 胸腔
- **sadness** [`sædnɪs] 哀傷

19

p. 39

突然間，奧菲斯有個開心的想法。
如果他演奏的歌曲夠悲傷，
或許可以讓妻子還魂。
世上的萬物都被他的音樂所感染，
但天上和冥界的神
還沒聽過他的音樂。

- **occur** [əˋkɝ] 想到
- **play with** [pleɪ wɪð]
  帶著……心情演奏
- **perhaps** [pəˋhæps] 也許
- **give back** [gɪv bæk]
  送回；歸還
- **live on** [lɪv ɑːn]
  在……居住
- **affected** [əˋfɛktɪd]
  受影響的

---

p. 40

既然尤麗黛去了冥界，
奧菲斯也決定前去。
他來到守誓河，
很溫和地用音樂說服了擺渡者，
讓他很快就擺渡過河到對岸。

當他遇到守護冥界大門的三頭犬時，
他彈起柔和的樂音，
讓三頭犬進入深深的睡眠中。

- **since** [sɪns] 從……之後
- **underworld** [ˋʌndəwɝːld]
  冥界；地獄
- **decide** [dɪˋsaɪd] 決定
- **arrive at** [əˋraɪv æt] 到達
- **gently** [ˋdʒɛntli]
  輕柔的；文雅的
- **persuade** [pəˋsweɪd]
  說服
- **ferryman** [ˋfɛrimæn]
  擺渡人
- **carry** [ˋkæri]
  把……帶到
- **reach** [riːtʃ] 到達；抵達
- **protect** [prəˋtɛkt] 守衛
- **relaxing** [rɪˋlæksɪŋ]
  使人懶洋洋的
- **fell into** [fɛl ˋɪntə]
  落入……；陷入……
  （fell的過去式）

20

p. 41

〔圖〕奧菲斯在冥王和冥后面前下跪

當他來到冥王和冥后面前時，
他跪了下來。
「歡迎你，奧菲斯！」冥王海地士說：
「起身。你就用唱的，
來告訴我們你此行的目的吧。」

- **stood before** [stʊd bɪˋfɔ:]
  站在……之前
  （stand的過去式）
- **Hades** [ˋheɪdi:z] 海地士
  （希神）
- **Persephone** [pəˋsɛfənɪ]
  泊瑟芬（希神）（冥王海
  地士之妻）
- **fell to one** [fɛll tə wʌn]
  跪著（祈禱；懇求）
- **rise** [raɪz] 起身；起立

---

p. 42

奧菲斯於是悲傷地唱著：
「喔！
慈者海地士，
人必來見你。
我日後身亡，
將回來此地。

- **sadly** [ˋsædli] 悲傷地
- **following** [ˋfɑ:ləʊɪŋ]
  接著的；下述的
- **words** [wɜ:d]
  話語；字詞
- **must** [məst] 必須
- **return to** [rɪˋtɜ:n] 返回
- **die** [daɪ] 死亡的
- **come back** [kʌm bæk]
  回來

21

p. 43

吾妻尤麗黛，
因毒蛇之牙，
離開我身邊，
如此之殘酷。

她正值青春，
卻來到此地，
美麗的少婦，
英年便早逝。

待她晚年時，
她會再回來。
但此時的她，
還屬於人間，
那凡人之地。

與妻子死別，
我無法獨活。
孤單的生活，
何等惹寂寞。」

- **has been taken from**
  [hæz biːn `teɪkən frəm]
  從……被奪走
- **snake's tooth**
  [sneɪks tuːθ] 蛇的牙齒
- **as . . . as** [əz əz]
  如……一般……
- **cruel** [`kruːəl] 殘酷
- **while** [waɪl]
  在……的時候
- **prime** [praɪm]
  青春；盛時
- **in one's prime**
  [ɪn wʌns praɪm]
  在……的青春正盛時期
- **belong** [bɪ`lɑːŋ]
  屬於……
- **above** [ə`bʌv]
  在……之上
- **separate from**
  [`sepərɪt frəm]
  從……分開
- **cannot go on**
  [`kænət gəu ɑːn] 無法生
  存；無法繼續下去
- **alone** [ə`ləun]
  單獨的；僅只
- **lonely** [`ləunli]
  孤獨的；孤單的

p. 44

聽著奧菲斯的詩歌，
冥王和冥后留下了眼淚。
歌曲聲聲動人，字字眞誠，
連冥界之神，也不得不爲之動容。

海地士伸手拭去臉上的淚，
說道：「可惜尤麗黛如此早逝。
我允許你將她帶回人間。」

- **shed** [ʃed]
  流；使流下（眼淚）
- **every** [ˋevri] 每個；每一
- **was full of** [wəz ful ɑːv]
  充滿……
- **can not help but**
  [kən nɑːt help bət]
  無法克制
- **be moved (by)**
  [bi muːvd baɪ]
  被……感動
- **wiping** [waɪpɪŋ]
  擦去；抹去
  （wipe爲原形）
- **pity** [ˋpɪti] 同情；可憐
- **allow** [əˋlaʊ] 允許；應允

p. 45

「不過，有一個條件。」
海地士說：
「在你走出冥界之前，
你不能回頭看她。」

尤麗黛從眾鬼魂中出現，
她因爲腳受傷，
走起路來一跛一跛的。

- **condition** [kənˋdɪʃən]
  條件
- **until** [ʌnˋtɪl] 直到……時
- **came from** [keɪm frəm]
  從……回來（came是
  come的過去式）
- **ghost** [gəʊst] 鬼魂
- **limping with** [lɪmpɪŋ wɪð]
  用……一拐一拐的走
- **wounded** [ˋwuːndɪd]
  受傷的

p. 46

奧菲斯走在前面開路，
尤麗黛緊跟在後。
他不看對方，
只朝著人間的方向走，
他們最先是通過三頭犬，
接著再渡過守誓河。

- **lead** [lid] 帶領；領路
- **follow** [ˋfɑːlou] 跟隨
- **without** [wɪðˋaut]
  沒有……
- **each other** [iːtʃ ˋʌðə]
  互相；彼此
- **walked toward**
  [wɑːkd təˋwɔːd] 向……
  走；朝……走
- **the three-headed dog**
  [ðə θriː-ˋhedɪd dɑːg]
  三顆頭的狗

p. 47

終於，他們走到了最後一段路程。
奧菲斯不確定妻子是否還跟在後面，
但他記著海地士的話，
所以不能回頭看妻子。

- **finally** [ˋfaɪnəli]
  最後；最終
- **reach** [riːtʃ] 抵達（目標）
- **trail** [treɪl] 小徑；小道
- **sure** [ʃɔː] 確定的；確信的
- **remember** [rɪˋmembə]
  記得
- **look back** [luk bæk]
  回頭看

p. 48

就在他們快走回到人間時，
尤麗黛被鬆落的岩石給絆倒，
發出了害怕的驚嚇聲。

奧菲斯一焦急，就轉身回頭看她。
就在他們眼光交會之時，
尤麗黛就在奧菲斯眼前消失了。
這對情人連道別的機會都沒有。

---

p. 49

〔圖〕尤麗黛從奧菲斯的身旁消逝無蹤

- **nearly** [ˋnɪəlɪ]
  幾乎；差不多
- **top** [tɑ:p]
  最高的；頂端的
- **slip** [slɪp] 滑倒；滑跤
- **loose** [lu:s] 鬆動的
- **scream** [skri:m]
  （因恐怖而）尖聲喊叫
- **fright** [fraɪt]
  驚恐；駭人的
- **anxious** [ˋæŋkʃəs]
  憂慮的；急切的
- **as soon as** [əs su:n əz]
  一……就……
- **disappear from**
  [͵dɪsəˋpɪə frəm]
  從……消失
- **sight** [saɪt] 眼睛；視域
- **couple** [ˋkʌpəl]
  一對（夫妻；情侶）
- **even** [ˋi:vən] 甚至

25

p. 50

奧菲斯馬上追著她來到冥界。
他來到守誓河邊，
但擺渡者不再聽他的請求。
奧菲斯唱著他的悲歌，
擺渡者卻用棉花把耳朵塞住。

奧菲斯就這樣站在岸邊唱著悲歌，
整整唱了七天七夜。

- **immediately** [ɪˈmiːdiətli]
  即刻
- **plea** [pliː] 請求
- **plug** [plʌg] 插入
- **cotton** [ˈkɑːtn] 棉花
- **bank** [bæŋk] 河的兩岸
- **sorrowful** [ˈsɑːroʊfəl]
  使人悲傷的；惋惜的

p. 51

但擺渡者仍不聽他唱歌。
一陣子之後，
他的歌曲變得越來越苦悶。
他知道，沒有人正在聽他的音樂。
他唱完最後一曲悲憤之歌後，
便返回人間。

- **bitter** [ˈbɪtə]
  苦悶的；使人痛苦的
- **after some time**
  [ˈɑːftə səm taɪm]
  一段時間之後
- **knew** [nəʊ]
  知曉（know的過去式）
- **last** [lɑːst]
  最後的；最末了的
- **the living** [ðə lɪvɪŋ]
  活著的

p. 52

他回到家中之後，他變得憤世嫉俗，
他再也不歌頌大自然或愛情的美好，
相反地，他只唱命運的悲慘，
和神祇們的不公平。

有一天，
一群美麗的女子
在這位音樂家身旁坐下。

- **no longer** [nau lɑːŋə]
  沒多久
- **beauty** [ˋbjuːti] 美
- **instead** [ɪnˋsted]
  取而代之的
- **fate** [feɪt] 命運
- **unfair** [ʌnˋfeə]
  不公平的；不公正的
- **a group of** [ə gruːp ɑːv]
  一群……
- **beside** [bɪˋsaɪd]
  在……旁邊

-----

p. 53

一個女子說：「奧菲斯，
請你如往常般，為我們歌唱。
沒有你愉快的音符，
生活變得憂愁又無趣。
可否請你暫時忘掉尤麗黛？
我們難道不如她美麗迷人嗎？」
「什麼？」奧菲斯咆哮道：
「跟她一樣美麗迷人？才不呢！」

有一個女子聽了非常生氣，
便隨手撿起一支掃帚，
朝奧菲斯的頭上用力敲下去。
奧菲斯隨即應聲倒地。

- **special** [ˋspeʃəl] 特別的
- **dull** [dʌl]
  晦澀的；暗淡的
- **melody** [ˋmelədi] 曲調
- **forget** [fəˋget] 忘掉
- **for a little while**
  [fə ə ˋlɪtl waɪl]
  一下子（的時間）
- **charming** [ˋtʃɑːmɪŋ]
  迷人的；嬌媚的
- **shouted** [ʃautɪd]
  大聲叫喊
- **pick up** [pɪk ʌp] 撿起
- **broomstick** [ˋbruːmˌstɪk]
  掃帚
- **hit** [hɪt] 打；擊
- **collapse** [kəˋlæps]
  倒地不起

27

p. 54

沒多久，奧菲斯睜開雙眼，
他以為
他會看到氣憤的女子正在瞪著他看，
但他眼前看到的
竟是他的妻子尤麗黛。
這對戀人，他們在冥界重逢了。
置身在她懷裡，
奧菲斯忘卻了所有的痛苦。

- **after a few moments** [ˋɑːftə ə fjuː ˋməʊmənts] 幾分鐘之後
- **expect to** [ɪkˋspekt tə] 期待
- **stare** [steə] 盯；凝視
- **together** [təˋgeðə] 在一起
- **bitterness** [ˋbɪtənəs] 痛苦

---

p. 55

他忘了曾經唱過的憤怒之歌，
他只知道他是如此的幸福。
於是從此之後，
他只唱快樂的歌曲。

這就是為什麼現在在冥界裡，
總是縈繞著快樂溫柔的旋律
的原因了。

- **from that day** [frəm ðæt deɪ] 從那天起

閱讀測驗

Part1 　　　　　　　　阿波羅和達芬妮 → 58-59 頁

※閱讀下列問題並選出最適當的答案。

1. 那枝「神奇金箭」對阿波羅起了什麼作用？
   (A) 使他忘記了愛羅斯。
   (B) 使他愛上之後第一個見到的女子。
   (C) 讓他殺了邪惡的怪物。
   (D) 讓他射箭射得很直。　　　　　　　　答案 (B)

2. 那枝「神奇鉛箭」對達芙妮起了什麼作用？
   (A) 使她永遠對男人失去興趣。
   (B) 讓她跑進森林裡。
   (C) 讓她變得更美麗。
   (D) 讓她在森林裡笑得很大聲。　　　　　答案 (A)

29

3. 爲什麼潘紐士要達芬妮不要躲阿波羅？

(A) 因爲潘紐士想要娶個合適的人。

(B) 因爲潘紐士覺得會被拒絕。

(C) 因爲潘紐士擔心他的孫子。

(D) 因爲潘紐士覺得阿波羅是個適合達芬妮的人
　　選。

答案 (D)

4. 在故事的最後，達芬妮發生了什麼事？

She had become a tree. 她已經變成一顆樹。

※**閱讀下列問題並回答。**

1. 奧菲斯在他十歲生日時，收到了什麼樣的禮物？
    (A) 一株好樹。
    (B) 一組高爾夫球具。
    (C) 一把里拉琴。
    (D) 野馬的鬃毛。   答案 (C)

2. 尤麗黛是如何死去的？
    (A) 她從懸崖上墜落。
    (B) 她是餓死的。
    (C) 她是病死的。
    (D) 她是被毒蛇咬死的。   答案 (D)

3. 為什麼奧菲斯覺得他必須到冥界去？
   (A) 因為他覺得尤麗黛很寂寞。
   (B) 因為他想讓冥界的人哭泣。
   (C) 因為他想說服海地士讓他的妻子回到他身邊。
   (D) 因為冥界的神喜歡聽音樂。　　　　答案 (C)

4. 在什麼樣的條件下，奧菲斯得以把尤麗黛帶回去？
   (A) 一直到他們走出冥界之前，奧菲斯都不能看尤麗黛一眼。
   (B) 他們不能從地獄犬三頭犬身邊經過。
   (C) 他們不能牽手。
   (D) 奧菲斯不能再演奏音樂。　　　　答案 (A)

5. 奧菲斯在被掃帚擊中頭部之後，發生了什麼事？
   參考答案

   Orpheus immediately collapsed to the ground. 奧菲斯應聲倒地。

32

※閱讀下段文章，並討論之以下的問題。 ➡ 62-63 頁

……阿波羅越來越逼近，達芬妮開始祈禱。「親愛的父親，請幫助我。阿波羅就要追上我了。請你打開大地，將我藏匿其中，或是將我變成樹、變成石頭吧！」達芬妮一祈禱完畢，人突然停止下來。……達芬妮變成了一棵樹！……

1. 因為達芬妮的祈禱，潘紐士把女兒變成了一棵樹。如果你是潘紐士，你會怎麼做？

   參考答案

   I would make her love Apollo by putting a spell on Daphne.

   我會在她身上施個魔法，好讓她愛上阿波羅。

……她發出了害怕的驚嚇聲。奧菲斯一焦急，就轉身回頭看她。就在他們眼光交會之時，尤麗黛就在奧菲斯眼前消失了。這對情人連道別的機會都沒有。……

2. 尤麗黛因為奧菲斯看了他一眼，便消失不見了。如果你是奧菲斯，你會怎麼做？

   參考答案

   Instead of looking at Eurydice, I would ask her if she is all right.

   我不會去看她，而是問她有沒有事就好了。

黃道十二宮

黃道十二宮 ➜ 64~68 頁

「黃道帶」（zodiac）這個字源自希臘文，意指「動物的環狀軌道」。黃道帶的起源為何？在本篇裡，你將可以看到說明星座來源的希臘神話故事：

太陽（the Sun）、地球（the Earth）、牡羊座（the Ram）、金牛座（the Bull）、雙子座（the Twins）、巨蟹座（the Crab）、獅子座（the Lion）、處女座（the Virgin）、天秤座（the Balance）、天蠍座（the Scorpion）、射手座（the Archer）、摩羯座（the Goat）、寶瓶座（the Water Bearer）、雙魚座（the Fishes）。

1. Aries（the Ram）牡羊座
2. Libra（the Balance）天秤座
3. Taurus（the Bull）金牛座
4. Scorpio（the Scorpion）天蠍座
5. Gemini（the Twins）雙子座
6. Sagittarius（the Archer）射手座
7. Cancer（the Crab）巨蟹座
8. Capricorn（the Goat）摩羯座
9. Leo（The Lion）獅子座
10. Aquarius（the Water Bearer）寶瓶座
11. Virgo（the Virgin）處女座
12. Pisces（the Fishes）雙魚座

牡羊座（the Ram） 3.21-4.20

牡羊座源自於金羊毛的故事。白羊安全營救福里瑟斯，福里瑟斯把金羊獻祭給宙斯作爲回報，宙斯便將金羊形象化爲天上星座。

金牛座（the Bull） 4.21-5.20

金牛座源自於歐羅巴和公牛的故事。宙斯化身爲公牛，以便吸引歐羅巴，公牛載著歐羅巴跨海來到克里特島。宙斯將公牛的形象化爲星座，以爲紀念。

雙子座（the Twins） 5.21-6.21

雙子座源自於卡斯特與波樂克斯的故事。他們兩人爲孿生兄弟，彼此相親相愛。爲了紀念其兄弟情誼，宙斯將他們的形象化爲星座。

巨蟹座（the Crab）　6.22-7.22

巨蟹座源自於赫丘力的十二項苦差役。希拉派遣巨蟹前去殺害赫丘力，但是赫丘力在打敗九頭蛇之前，一腳將巨蟹踩碎。爲了紀念巨蟹，希拉將其形象化爲星座。

獅子座（The Lion）　7.23-8.22

獅子座亦源自於赫丘力十二項苦差中。赫丘力的第一項苦差，是要殺死奈米亞山谷之獅。他徒手殺了獅子，爲了紀念這項偉大的事蹟，宙斯將奈米亞獅子的形象，置於星辰之中。

處女座（the Virgin）　8.23-9.22

處女座源自於潘朵拉的故事。處女指的是純潔與天眞女神阿絲蒂雅。潘朵拉好奇將禁盒打開，讓許多邪惡事物來到人間，眾神紛紛返回天庭。爲了紀念這種失落的純眞，便把阿絲蒂雅的形象置於群星中。

天秤座（the Balance）　9.23-10.21

天秤是正義的秤子，由神聖正義女神蒂米絲隨身攜帶。天秤座落在處女座旁邊，因為阿絲蒂雅是蒂米絲之女。

天蠍座（the Scorpion）　10.22-11.21

天蠍座源自於歐里昂。歐里昂和阿蒂蜜絲是一對狩獵夥伴，阿蒂蜜絲的哥哥阿波羅對此忌妒不已。他請求蓋亞殺了歐里昂。因此，蓋亞創造天蠍殺了偉大的歐里昂。為了紀念此事，宙斯將歐里昂和天蠍化成星座。這兩個星座從來不會同時出現。

射手座（the Archer）　11.23-12.21

射手座代表卡隆。在希臘神話故事中，卡隆是許多英雄的朋友，例如亞吉力、赫丘力。赫丘力以毒箭誤傷了卡隆。卡隆是神，因此得以不死，但是卻必須忍受這無止盡的痛苦，所以卡隆央求宙斯殺了他。為了紀念卡隆，宙斯將他化為星座。

摩羯座（the Goat） 12.22-1.19

魔羯代表哺育年幼宙斯的羊阿瑪爾夏。
據說宙斯為了感念此羊，將之化為星座。

寶瓶座（the Water Bearer） 1.20-2.18

寶瓶座源自於鐸卡連的洪水。在這個故事中，宙
斯在人間降下豪雨，讓洪水沖走一切邪惡的生
物。只有鐸卡連和妻子皮雅是洪水的生還者。

雙魚座（the Fishes） 2.19-3.20

雙魚座代表愛與美之女神阿芙柔黛蒂，
以及其子愛神愛羅斯。當時有個颶風，
兩人沿著優芙瑞特河步行。他們請求宙
斯援救，宙斯將兩人變成魚，讓他們安
然渡過風災。為了紀念此事，阿芙柔黛
蒂化身為星座中的大魚，愛羅斯則化為
小魚。

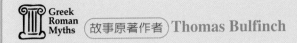

Without a knowledge of mythology much of the elegant literature of our own language cannot be understood and appreciated.

缺少了神話知識，就無法了解和透徹語言的文學之美。

—*Thomas Bulfinch*

Thomas Bulfinch（1796-1867），出生於美國麻薩諸塞州的Newton，隨後全家移居波士頓，父親爲知名的建築師Charles Bulfinch。他在求學時期，曾就讀過一些優異的名校，並於1814年畢業於哈佛。

畢業後，執過教鞭，爾後從商，但經濟狀況一直未能穩定。1837年，在銀行擔任一般職員，以此爲終身職業。後來開始進一步鑽研古典文學，成爲業餘作家，一生未婚。

1855年，時值59歲，出版了奠立其作家地位的名作*The Age of Fables*，書中蒐集希臘羅馬神話，廣受歡迎。此書後來與日後出版的 *The Age of Chivalry*（1858）和 *Legends of Charlemagne*（1863），合集更名爲 *Bulfinch's Mythology*。

本系列書系，即改編自 *The Age of Fable*。Bulfinch 著寫本書時，特地以成年大眾爲對象，以將古典文學引介給一般大眾。*The Age of Fable* 堪稱十九世紀的羅馬神話故事的重要代表著作，其中有很多故事來源，來自Bulfinch自己對奧維德（Ovid）的《變形記》（*Metamorphoses*）的翻譯。

■Bulfinch 的著作

1. Hebrew Lyrical History.
2. The Age of Fable: Or Stories of Gods and Heroes.
3. The Age of Chivalry.
4. The Boy Inventor: A Memoir of Matthew Edwards, Mathematical-Instrument Maker.
5. Legends of Charlemagne.
6. Poetry of the Age of Fable.
7. Shakespeare Adapted for Reading Classes.
8. Oregon and Eldorado.
9. Bulfinch's Mythology: Age of Fable, Age of Chivalry, Legends of Charlemagne.